Lucius and the Storm

Written and Illustrated by
Kent Knowles

red
cygnet™
PRESS

San Diego, California

To Katherine, my love and inspiration. – K.K.

Illustrations copyright © 2007 Kent Knowles
Manuscript copyright © 2007 Kent Knowles
Book copyright © 2007 Red Cygnet Press, Inc., 11858 Stoney Peak Dr. #525, San Diego, CA 92128

Cover and book design: Amy Stirnkorb

First Edition 2007
10 9 8 7 6 5 4 3 2
Printed in China

Library of Congress Cataloging-in-Publication Data

Knowles, Kent.
Lucius and the storm / written and illustrated by Kent Knowles. -- 1st ed.
p. cm.
Summary: Brave and bold, young Lucius battles Old Man Weather in an effort to save summer vacation.
ISBN-13: 978-1-60108-005-9 (hardcover)
ISBN-10: 1-60108-005-0 (hardcover)
[1. Weather--Fiction. 2. Vacations--Fiction. 3. Stories in rhyme.] I. Title.
PZ8.3.K751137Lu 2007
[E]--dc22
2006017852

Far from the tree line
Where the hillsides are black
Past the crooked red river
Near the tall smoking stack

Through
glimmering branches
And shining rock
Where owls look backward
And pigeons flock

High on a hill
Of petrified Spruces
With a stone in his hand
Stands the brave, bold,
young Lucius.

He's watching the sky
As deep shadows pass
When the sunlight yields
To a cumulus mass

A tremendous
black cloud,
Wet and consuming,
With one terrible purpose
Lurking and looming

To plunge sunny Summer
Headlong into dark,
To scatter the bushes
And wash out the park

To crack the trees
And tip the cattle
To make rooftops whistle
And cupboards rattle

To jumble the trains
And blow all their fuses,
Everyone's scared
Except brave, young Lucius

He peers at the monster
Now consuming the sky
At Old Man Weather
And his one cobalt eye.

Could it be this gray beast
Will last the duration?
And claim the remains
Of Summer Vacation?

Would there be no more fishing
At Hangman's Creek?
Or noonday picnics
At the Widow's Peak?

And what of the balloon rides
He takes with his cat?
Surely the storm
Wouldn't dare threaten that.

"No," thinks brave Lucius,
"This simply won't stand"
As he clutches a stone
That rests in his hand.

Fixing his gaze
On the black darkened form
Lucius decides
He will conquer the storm

So with calm careful aim
He raises his fist
And heaves the great stone
At the mischievous mist.

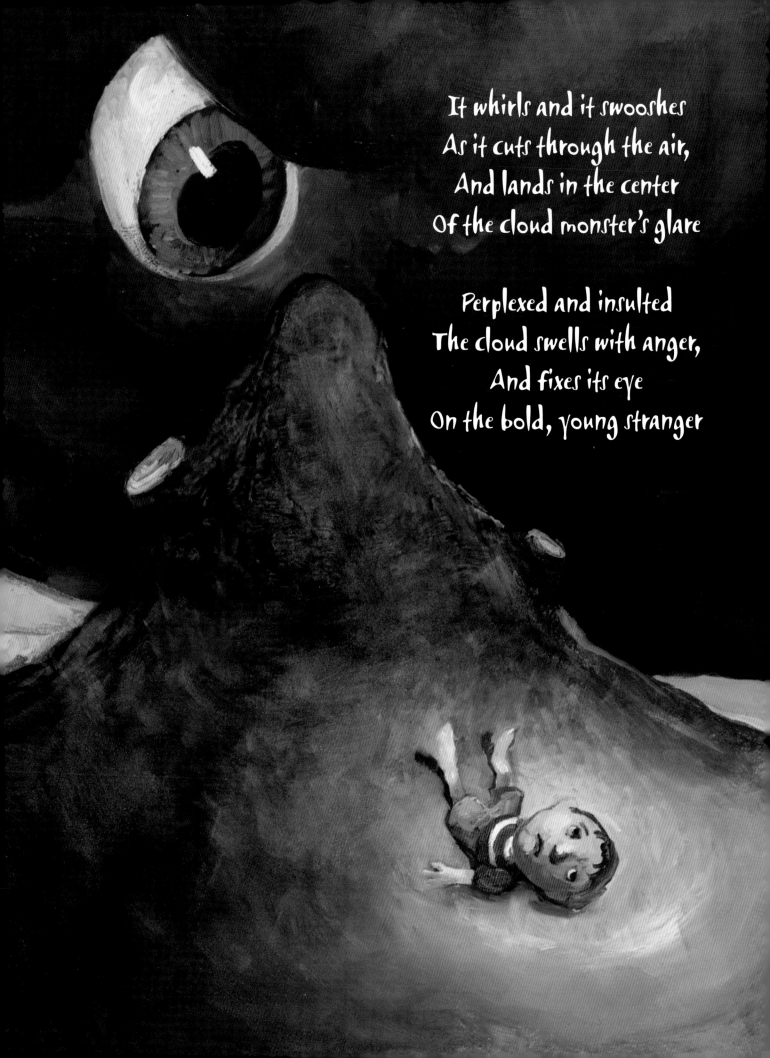

It whirls and it swooshes
As it cuts through the air,
And lands in the center
Of the cloud monster's glare

Perplexed and insulted
The cloud swells with anger,
And fixes its eye
On the bold, young stranger

With a deafening groan
In a watery wave,
The sky rains down
On young Lucius, the brave

With a thunderous boom
And a clamorous spill,
The young boy is pushed
To the low of the hill

His body is tossed
And rolled in the dirt,
Everything's soaked
From his shoes to his shirt

The satisfied storm
Black, moist, and round
Laughs at young Lucius,
Lying wet on the ground

And feeling quite certain
That he'd beaten the pest,
The storm spreads its arms
To the fields in the West

Alone in a puddle
Lucius wonders aloud,
"How was I beaten
By a sniveling cloud?"

And what of the Sun,
Where was he through all this?
Had he cowardly fled
Before things went amiss?

And just as brave Lucius
Is thinking all this,
The tall smoking stack
Gives a wonderful hiss

The exterior bricks,
In their youth straight and pink,
Are now tattered and slimy
And beginning to stink

No one recalls
Just when it was built,
Generations have choked
On its shadowy silt

And though long abandoned
It remains quite intact,
Such is the resolve
Of the tall smoking stack.

A curious Lucius
Approaches the stack,
Where an iron gate smiles
As its hinges re-crack

And lo', at the base
Of the dark looming turret,
A small door swings open,
Though the rain tries to blur it

A sheltering hatch
Through which Lucius can crawl,
Safe from the whistle
Of the monster's wet squall

Blindly, he darts,
Like a rabbit to a hole,
Jumping head first
Through a cavern of coal

There's a SPLOOSH! as he lands
In a greasy tailspin,
Groping the void
Of the dark smoking den

And then, just as quickly
As it opened before,
A force closes shut
The shiny hatch door

His eyes strain to adjust
To the formless cold dark,
As Lucius is greeted
By a lone, crimson spark

Glowing and growing
And warming the space
Now flames lick the contours
Of Lucius's face

As the chamber becomes
Slowly illumined,
A whisper emerges
It sounds almost human.

"Are you comfortable?"
The voice inquires

"Closer, boy!"
The flame grows loud,
"Are you the young one
Making war with the cloud?"

"Are you volleying stones
At the clattering sky,
And thumbing your nose
At the tempest's one eye?"

A reluctant wet Lucius
Chilled to the bone,
Considers the fire
And its curious tone

With gentle, small steps
He approaches the flame
Then the shivering boy
Announces his name

"Yes, it is I
Throwing rocks at the storm."
At this the flame wiggles
And takes a new form.

Swelling its heat
To a hot brilliant red,
The fire takes shape
As a torso and head

"I've watched armies of men
Raise their swords to the mist,
With scowls on their faces
And guns in their fists"

"Many boys just like you,"
Said the fiery form,
"Have long tried to topple
This ancient cruel storm"

"Catapults, bombs
Every kind of contraption,
But no means have brought
Men much satisfaction"

"And yet..."
The flames now
begin to sing,
"All one really needs..."
Is one simple thing"

As if savoring a punch line
From a favorite joke,
She leans in toward Lucius
And starts whispering,
"SSS...SMOKE."

Meanwhile... the storm
Squats hard on the day,
Stretching from townships
To the warm, salty bay

The selfish, smug storm,
Content with his mess,
Feels there is no one
Left to impress.

Then a curious thing,
A column of soot
Appears with a head
And a tapered black foot

It comes from the mouth
Of the tall smoking stack,
It moves like a train
On a twisted puff'd track

Deep at the heart
Of this billowing pyre,
A boy shovels coal
On a ravenous fire

"More!" the flame shouts
In hysterical joy,
While hope floods the heart
Of the shoveling boy

An explosion of smoke
Bursts up through the stack,
And blows a huge hole
In the monster's moist back

The gray of the cloud
Turns a fiery brown,
As pieces of storm
Fall fast to the ground

The storm reels backward
From the crippling blow,
As the flame in the chimney
Continues to grow

Its wrath now awakened
The cloud gathers its storms
And into a huge raging
Twister transforms

The wet, heaving mass
Of the monstrous cloud,
Forms into a funnel
Angry and loud

The cloud
cracks a hole
In the side
of the stack,
As the billowing
bloom
Turns the dark
gray sky, black

The enemies merge
As the battlefield
shrinks,
Dark bricks
are shattered
As the heavy
cloud sinks

The poisoned storm then
Careens to the ground,
Reducing the stack
To a short smoking mound

A hiss then escapes
From the dusty shroud,
And covers the carcass
Of the fallen cloud.

A cackle is heard
On the ghost of a breeze,
As the embers all fade
Over swollen burnt trees

The hillside is broken
And the tundra burns,
As the soft, yellow face
Of the sunlight returns

And the brightness of Summer
Laying claim to the moor,
Turns a delicate ear
To a tiny hatch door

And lo' from a portal
At the ruin's burned base,
A figure emerges
From a darkened crawl space.

Lifting his head
To welcome the day
The young man
searches
For a good place
to play

He re-takes his place
At the top of the hill
Where he first
raised his fist
And gathered his will

He soaks up
the sunshine
And slowly gets warm,
He smiles to himself,
He's conquered
the storm.